I0676789

Don't Quote Me on That

Written By:

Jamie Aldridge

"The man who does not read
has no advantage over the man
who cannot read."
                    -Mark Twain

Quiet

Down
Town
Frown wearing metrifiers
Jack ass people wearing the biggest disasters
Silence works best with internal laughter

Triple Rainbow

He hopped to and frow
He leaped over every bad angle
He found out how to sleep
He jumped up behind me
He framed all their misery

Help Them Not Die

Can't you see them crying?
Can't you hear them suffering?
Can't you feel their pain?
Can't you cover up their shame with rain?
Can't you feed their soul with love?
Can't you wait until they stop bleeding?

Must you judge their season?
Must you take their hope cake away?
Must you walk all over their inherent value?
Must you take their last dollar?
Must you fail to say a proper prayer for them?
Must you laugh at what's killing them?

Don't you care when people eat themselves alive?
Don't you stop when their face turns blue?
Don't you leap with them across bounds?
Don't you feel what keeps them awake at night?
Don't you have more than your fair share?
Don't you want them to be saved too?

Why is it only ever about you?

Moving

Day
Parts
Cars
Hearts
Planes
Dirt
Rooms
Clouds
Towns
Sounds
Ground
Chairs
Close
Accounts
Offices
Pictures
Again
Away

Shake Me Free

From who I used to be
From who I want to be
From what they speak of me
From who sat on top of me
From the rotten Adam's apple
From yeast infections from the deep
From New Year's monopoly
From living above my means
From lying pterodactyls
From crying slabs of meat
From Chinese made ashes
From hormonal Septembers
From crying laughter
From saggy ball sacks
From sinister apple pie
From visceral fat

Fondue Songs

Cry me a river
Put a ring on it
Honey sugar baby
Kissed by a rose
Hit me baby one more time

54th Street

Miracles
Testicles
Receptacles
Phony nuptials
Expensive facials
Finger service
Green origami
Buckled ovaries
Diverse sexuality
Vaginal wish lists
Buy me this, that, and the other
Home to joint investment
Foreign pimps living forever
Moms who are still alive
Smoke screens everywhere

Cereal

Bowl, spoon, milk
Crunchy, soggy, sugar
Scrumptious, satisfying, stellar
Fun, flavors, forever
Babies, kids, adults
Eyes, mouth, spirit
Clang, slurp, savor
Dry, wet, drenched
Mix, match, solo
Topping, entrée, dessert

But, You Did

Didn't mean to
Wasn't my intent
I meant something else
Well, you said it first
I forgot about it
My heart was in the right place
Other people did it too
There wasn't another option
You didn't notice last time
It was just a joke
It's not that big of a deal

Your Job

Your start
Your supplies
Your trash
Your pet
Your weight
Your taxes
Your teeth
Your laundry
Your mother
Your bills
Your hair
Your yard
Your mouth
Your anger
Your participation
Your reputation
Your success
Your heart
Your finish

Go

Now
Or else
That's it
I'm done
It's finished
Time's up
Say goodbye
Pull the plug
Over there
You will find
Home

Mad Sick

Lightning strikes
Jerks unite
Leopard's spit
Sick of this shit

Grandma bakes
Worker's strike
Homeless tricks
Sick of this shit

Fearless tongues
Pregnant trash
Busted ganache
Sick of this shit

Fingers raised
Maturity rapes
Literal waste
Sick of this shit

Endless blame
Crime glorified
Tolerance justified
Sick of this shit

Morning Meds

Bubble gum Brenda
Ten cups of coffee John
Matcha Martha
Natural riser Steve
Smokey Dave
Green smoothie Liam
Elijah runs hard
Quiet time Kendra
Hot shower Sally
Singing Trevor
Donut Debra
Choo-choo

Goodnight Pills

Mary Jane
Tom Melatonin
Harry Nyquil
Jenny Tonic
Midnight Sara
Xanax Charlie
T.V. Tanisha
Mr. Magnesium
Rain Thompson
Shopping Joneses
Word Whores
Zzz

It Gets Worse

The more you know,
the less we own

No one is completely free,
nor fully in tune with reality

Make the bullets free,
so we can die on top of things

Read Wine

Wine and book talks
Wine while you cook
Wine watch parties
Wine meetings
Wine baths
Wine clubs
Wine tours
Wine music
Wine weddings
Wine at the funeral
Wine walks
Wine down

Fucking Gross

All the dust
All the polluted air
All the water snakes
All the cobwebs
All the toe jam
All the fake nails
All the fake spider eyelashes
All the poop remnants
All the gingivitis
All the mayonnaise on it
All the hair on it
All the lemon drop vomit
All the bald cats
All the broken vaginas
All the cloudy water
All the brown stains
All the naked monkeys
All the bruised faces
All the flat asses
All the immature laughter
All the porn fanatics

Take Me with Hue

Sometimes I'm blue with unexplainable black depression
Sometimes I'm green with purple past discretions
Sometimes I'm red with yellow manic depression
Sometimes I'm silver with sunny orange organic
impulsivity
Sometimes I'm gray with brown self-righteous
indignation
Sometimes I'm black with white emotional
claustrophobia
Sometimes I'm pink with abundant rainbow acceptance

Elvis Impressley

Why you dressed so fancy?
You're making me look less than ghetto
How about we polish our nails exactly?
Next, we'll tackle semantics
Let's be equally sintastic
I really wish you looked less fantastic
Maybe I should put you on a leash so you can't leave
Hold my hand ever so firmly
Lead me into stoic ecstasy
I can't help falling in love with your immortal poison

Uncle Bentley

Please wake him ever so gently
His refrigerator stays open longer than most
Watch out for his manipulative dimples
He spends more than the government makes
His name opens the door to causation
He has never graced a steepled building
He likes to ask for help popping his butt pimples
He babysits for free
He is nowhere near obsolete

Allowances

You can go home whenever you want
You cannot take me with you
You can eat whatever you want
You cannot force me to eat anything
You can buy clothes that don't fit
You cannot convince me your clothes actually fit
You can drink as much as you dare to
You cannot open up a random can of whoop ass on me

You will get old
You won't always be happy
You will get in serious trouble
You won't be able to weasel your way out of it
You will drown if you don't swim
You won't laugh when the joke stings
You will be confused
You won't take me down with you

Fried Food

Greasy for caloric reasons
Serves as a dopamine diuretic
Poses as a leaf racing with the wind
Contains finger licking poison
Explains why he'd rather just shave it bald
Allows for a repeat coping mechanism
Kills mental stamina
Violates right and wrong
Provides a vacation for all seasons
Creates dents all over the planet
Leaves you no longer horny

That's What He Said

No
Go
Hoe
Mow
Stop
Gold
Digger
Enter
Please
Believe
Lies
Fine
Why
I
Don't
Give
Two
Shits

Spread It

News
Blues
Legs
Kegs
Butter
Clutter
Disease
Unease
Love
Clove
Fragrance
Impatience
Gestation
Innovation
Viruses
Afflatus
Laughter
Water
Darkness
Surprises

POV:

I swear
I promise
I never
I didn't
I wouldn't
I pretended
I lied
I left
I forgot

You said it
You broke it
You were there
You drove
You did it
You messed up
You saw it
You drank it

We went
We laughed
We ignored
We stole
We failed
We got lost
We ignored it
We died trying

Dumb Fucks

Mess shit up
Blow your cover
Drive all over every lane
Waste your time
Talk you into crazy
Suck at do overs
Stick their nose in your business
Piss off empathetic people
Can't get out of the way
Kill good vibes
Look for ways to die
Make you want to fry their eyes
Will always stick around

Little People

Bite their nails
Walk belly out
Smell like jail
Can't see past their feet
Quit growing in middle school
Wait for you to crack first
Jump out of their truck
Read the news first
Never find true love
Think they are a home run
Aren't worth one second of your time
Cry when they don't get their way
Melt at the sight of hard work
Drink decaf to feel better on the outside
Love when it's your fault
Vanish if you call their number
Believe they're taller than reality
Fake big people energy

Tell Me Less

About your boob job
About your three cats
About what you ate for dinner
About your favorite female body part
About how much money you have
About the latest video game that you played
About what you want to be when you grow up
About why you still live at home
About why you dropped out of college
About your favorite football team
About how many beers you drank
About your ten kids
About your broken childhood
About why your breath stinks
About why you're overweight
About why you overslept
About why you lied again
About how many friends you have
About how hot she is
About your first car
About why you yelled
About when you lost your virginity
About your facial hair that you can't grow
About how much money you donated
About the time you almost cried in public
About how little the stick is
About your obsession with bacon
About the day you got married
About the car wreck that changed your life
About how important you are

Popcorn Glares

Smell the butter lubing their juvenile arteries
Find their momma nowhere in sight
Endless soda fountain runs for the extra chubby ones
Hear their ruthless smacking cracking away at your
peace
Watch them not even give a damn who's around
Regret your life decisions in the dark
Let them ruin the entire movie
Realize that popcorn has no limits
Give them the go to hell look at least ten times
Leave questioning why some people were invented

Block Em

Done talking
Bye-bye chances
Out of forgiveness
Over their nonsense
Forever regretting their faces
No longer will they get anything from you
Say I don't need this
Repeat the million reasons not to need them
They don't deserve an explanation
Ghosting is how you make them nameless

Full Moon

All you want
All you need
All who believe
All who see
All the trees
All the leaves
All we can do
All we can be
All in
All out
All gone
All here
All over
All under
All matter
All commit sins
All are still welcome
All are set free
All is enough
All aboard

Hard

Knocks
Rocks
Times
Rhymes
Crimes
Fines
Hearts
Parts
Turns
Sounds
Facts
Money
Answer
Boundaries
Date
Face
Race
Ground
Day
Life

Seriously

Shut up
Sit down
Stand by
Save face
Sing louder
Swim faster
Suck harder
Stop laughing
Save it
Stalk him
Strip less
Sink further
Sip strategically
Spank them
Smell better

Good

Apple
Man
Grief
Dream
News
Booze
Gracious
Name
Game
Side
Excuse
Friend
Try
Cry
Life
Talk
Wifi
Deal

Son of a Good Mom

He has selfless manners
He has a solid work ethic
He takes pride in an honest reputation
He takes golden opportunities to make provision
He says sorry without conditions
He says sorry without apprehension
He owns real estate
He owns his bank
He knows her without her saying
He knows without repercussion
He shows love in the moment
He shows love like a grown up
He listens generously
He listens to learn
He feels bad when others fail
He feels sad when he can't fix it

Son of A Bad Mom

He lacks chivalry
He lacks awareness
He doesn't work hard
He doesn't care about others
He yells at women
He lies to himself
He cries when he is told no
He cries when he loses control
He drives like a bat out of hell
He drives over right and wrong
He sends mixed signals
He sends people to mental prisons
He laughs at boundaries
He laughs at undeniable truths
He wears clothes that don't fit
He wears invisible shame

Unconventional

In the nose
In the butt
In the ear
From the stairs
From the bush
From the trampoline
On the elbow
On the chin
On the moose knuckle
Back hand
Side tongue
Three thumbs
You scream
I cry
We never die
Dessert fries
Golden lies
Millennial roads
Closed eyes
Humming to apple pie

Le Marhoe

They suck their own toes
They mail black stars to the sky
They play guitars with their eyes
They sleep their way into penthouse views
They show more skin than a sphynx cat
They eat dynamite in between drinks
They leave you dirtier than before
They prey on sleeping sloppy souls
They cry tears from the top of the well
They belong in the Kentucky Derby

Nasty Twat

You can't hide in a thong
You can't ride all night long
You can't spit on everyone's face
You can't get asked out on a second date
You can't kegel a bald eagle
You should befriend a good douche
You should try to become tight as a noose
You should wash off the moose
You should bleed into your own shoes
You should sniff what you're selling
You should be foreclosed on

Salut

I hope you miss me
I hope you flinch when you think of my name
I hope you're sorry for being so lame
I hope your pants sink to your lying feet in public
I hope you realize my laugh,
was not an ounce next to insane
I hope you regret calling my bluff
I hope God forgives your style of crying
I hope it's my face you see in the breeze
I hope you choke on the food I didn't make
I hope you lament second guessing my health
Bon débarras

We Can't Be Friends

You remind me of them
I remind you of them
Sharing isn't always because you care
They remain and I left for Maine
It's best we part leaving the elephant in the room
Justification makes none of us even
Go your way and I'll find mine
Occupy the same old streets
Linger with beer covered singers
I'll be busy in more appropriate company
Good thing we can forget
Stay cool
Have fun
Best wishes
Don't be dumb

Uber Times

Dashes showing crashes
Smells airing lazy laundry
Wheels of undone matrimony
Tanks of empty Christmases
Seat belts with no other option
Musical cushion for judging
Drivers with slimy credentials
Trunks closed for spiritual business

Cry Me A Sorry River

Never again
Don't even think about it
Stay in your lane
Talk to the ghost
Be gone before my next toast

Tom, Dick, and Hairy

Walk leaning
Walk rubbing
Walk chubbing
Walk throbbing
Walk shrinking
Walk drooling
Walk fooling
Walk small
Walk medium
Walk big
Walk insecure
Walk unsure
Walk proud
Walk alone
Walk present
Walk consumed
Walk away

Like

This is how I talk
I say "like"
Like, in between every other word

How do you like how I talk?
Like, do you love me already?
Like, it's been two days since I ate

Like, can you like my post?
Like, I don't know why it's so cold
Like, this dude cat called me
He's like such a like total douche

Like, my mom's such a bitch
Like, I ate like trash last night
Like, what the hell was he thinking?

For real, like money doesn't like make you happy
For real, like you're not even my boss

Like, that's why I like don't even like you

Lost Dawgs

Drinking for thrills
Can't pay the bills
Smoking for escape
Barely know their own name
Always wearing heavy chains
Comprised mostly of bones jointed to shame
They will not come when you call their name
They are the best at playing dead

Dainty Lil Thang

He winks, she blinks
He stinks, she thinks

He dreams, she believes
He talks, she walks

He sells, she sails
He splashes, she dives

He connives, she bereaves
He slaves, she saves

He fabricates, she finds
He blinds, she reminds

He undoes, she gloves
He dies, she cries

Back Seat

Driver
Shenanigans
Pinch arounds
Naps
Slaps
Views
Friends
Tension
Flirting
Babies
Games
Suffocating
Criminals
Animals

Certain Folks

They don't come in one shade
They don't have easy names
They embrace dry skin
They self-segregate
They live loudly
They rap soulfully
They exchange rowdy energy
They eat vivaciously
They fight for individuality
They speak their own language
They dance naturally
They laugh for money
They die for profanity
They don't desire reality
They live in hypersensitivity

Couples

Fight	Love	Manipulate
Cheat	Triumph	Gripe
Scream	Reproduce	Complain
Leave	Give	Situate
Laugh	Resent	Listen
Dance	Withhold	Linger
Sing	Procrastinate	Uplift
Believe	Isolate	Validate
Hit	Kiss	Wound
Curse	Bliss	Wallow
Lie	Miss	Waiver
Deny	Wish	Sever
Provide	Hate	Serenade
Dream	Wait	Savor
Travel	Irritate	Surrender
Grow	Postulate	Share
Blame	Help	Slander
Shame	Sacrifice	Enslave
Devalue	Compromise	Erupt
Abandon	Celebrate	Enrage

Oystares

All the states
All the eye balls
All the games
All the mistakes
All the fingers
All the frowns
All the invisible crowns
All the furled brows
All the full tongues
All the swallowed names
All the fun afterward

Farmer's Smarket

Smells for every scent
Tastes for finnicky friends
Piss on every come again
Wish you enjoyed big girls
Find food for thoughtless oblivion
Laugh when dogs say ah-choo
Wonder how people ever came about
Realize how much things are worth

Print Her

Paper people
Labels
Connection unstable
Ink
Fades to gray
The jam remains unfixable
Two sides to every copy
Collate and staple her
Never emasculate her quality
Empty her old trays
Reinstate blame copies
Scan her name twice
Refresh her page
Press her and cancel the job
Queue what's new
Restore her properties

Dirty Shoes

You have walked more than a mile or two through the
mud of life
There have always been bigger fish to fry
You are not well to do
Your laces have always been over extended
You are indolent when it comes to personal aesthetics
You have squandered life itself
You go places no fowl would fish
You take reckless dreams for real
You lean on your own understanding
You need a new lease on former life
You are the problem
You forget where you've been and how far you've come
You don't know a single reason why

Come Again

There will never be soul mates
We walk on dry water
She left her brains in his pants
Today is the only tomorrow
Crying is not just for babies
Friendships don't rely on trust
The best part of the pizza is the crust
Cinderella would be better off alone
Grandpa requests to die in his chair
The best trash can is your hair
Jealous people invented the glare
Serendipity is when you feel nippy
Tank tops don't work for every body
Grass is green as long as you water it
Self-prison has no release date
It makes no difference who you vote for
Time always tells on you
Hair is the proverbial ghost writer
A house is home when you die in it

About To Snap

Shut up
Be quiet
Simmer down
Police yourself
Back up
Hold up
Here we go
Hey now
Slow your roll
Chill
Think about it
Get a grip
Check yourself
Remember what shatters
Make the last laugh matter
Row your boat home
Tame the tongue
Silence the bees
Just breathe
Time out
Pause
Walk away

Gold Dust

Have no fear, there's always more beer
Talk is cheap, so listen to their feet
Men are supposedly all bad, while women trust in fads
Clean up after yourself, but leave room for snoozing
Walk away or you'll become their chore

Taken

So long
So much
So wrong
So early
So abruptly
So seriously
Enough

What's In Front of Me?

Daddy's big deal
Momma's cheap thrills
Sandy's white van
Leondra's huge donkey
Trees with only nocturnal leaves
Conundrums of the men who didn't care to sleep with
you
Fantastic teenagers headed to the slammer
My grandpa's generational led cigar
Mr. Miyagi's mystery moves
Lunch with those still learning how to accept an allegory
Stairs to open gluten morphology
Hair that freaks people on the stairs
Conceptualization of her chubby knees
Salty shores with cerebral energy
Oppositional bending over
Smurfs disguised in chocolate
Ten people wondering what's for dinner

When We Kiss

The love should feel electric
The lips should taste loyal
The duration will always depend
The setting shall be everchanging
The reflections must produce a smile
The last one leaves room for the next one
The eyes stay closed in delightment
The chemistry will make problems no longer matter

Zoo Disaster

Hippos smoking snake lungs
Elephants wearing giraffe leg belts
Black bears humping white apes
Flamingos flying on monkey faces
Penguins parading around fish poop
Children drowning under Tiger's Crossing
Parents losing the zoo keepers marbles
Water gushing all the way up to the eagles
Fish swimming into the restroom urinals
Security intoxicated at the exits
Rainchecks only for the toothless
Animal scented candles in the giftshop
Free memories that make you want to die
Come again when it's time to raise your blood pressure

Talking Pianos

Keys telling me who to sleep with
Benches holding their tongue
Pedals sustaining feet only after extensions
Music shelves with scripted directions
Side arms suggesting I lose weight
Bass strings surrounded by hammered friends
Casters rolling me into more debt
The bridge poses as my soundboard
Their only goal is lifting my grand cabinet

Drives Me

Home
Mad
Wild
Crazy
Nuts
Out of my mind

Flies Me

Away
Smooth
Through
Over
Around
To the moon

Toast To Nobody Knows

I counted his toes before he made me holler
He laser beamed my clothes right off me
I ripped his beneath the waist beard
He whipped my face with white marks of disaster
I traced his butt all the way home from Mrs. Baird's
He fingered me with money from Monopoly
I stretched my tongue across more than his inches
He wrote my name on a fallen crown
Nostrovia

Honk If

You see me
You need me
You have anger problems
You are annoying
You think I am slow
You read my bumper
You love me
You can't stand me
You think I'm wrong
You drank too much
You fell asleep at the wheel
You want what you can't have
You are impatient
You are oblivious
You don't know how to use words

How Much?

What does it cost to divorce you?
What does it actually mean to your dog?
What does it matter that I don't want to dance with you?
Why does it smell when they half-way ghost you?
Why do they drink all alone?
Why do they cry at the sight of you?
Why is there pee beyond the trees?
Who made them jump off the authenticity cliff?

Seeping In

Today's not the way
You can't buy your
friends
My love hides her den
I wish I could win
Yet, sad comes instead

Seeping in times ten
Friends that never knew
Love that poisons sin,
poisons sin deep within
Seeping in, seeping in

One day they will know
Truth trumps depression
For now, sad reigns
within
Take me down memory
lane
We might just delay
pain

Seeping in times ten
Weeping to fallen
friends
Dreaming of calm
waters
Topping off blood
cheers
Seeping in, seeping in

Taming the flesh flakes,
is a full-time job
I should fire myself
How can I care more?
Souls find corruption

Tell me the way out
Seeping in, seeping in
One more pretend kiss
Look beyond the scar
Seeping in, seeping in

Sounds Fun

I'm chewing gum backwards
I'm twerking on Tik-Tok in yellow spandex
I'm eating while sleeping
I'm drinking milk next to a cow
I'm shaking hands with their prosthetic
I'm racing nude across the finish line
I'm liking all the depressing photos
I'm branding everyone as free
I'm groping the bottom of the banana tree
I'm mashing the potatoes with my fists
I'm climbing over the great wall of China
I'm pushing people to their unholy limits
I'm driving drunk people home

Not Fun

Falling down
Breaking your neck
Bending your stick
Loving those who don't give a flip
Eating finger foods without fingers
Drinking applesauce straight up
Waking up from a bad dream
Slipping into the wrong hole
Grabbing more than you can carry
Opening the door on your foot
Squeezing the wrong end of the tube
Believing their lies more than twice
Thinking they intended to be loyal
Putting your faith in man
Wishing they would be different
Running out of toilet paper
Overpaying Uncle Sam
Taking the long way down
Jumping in head first
Mixing business with family
Dressing casual to their funeral
Sleeping past noon
Freezing beside cold hearts
Lapping yourself in the pantry
Losing all that you put in

Not My Name

Amy
Tammy
Janie
James
Jimmy

Let Me

Pray
Drool
Sleep
Crawl
Drown
Fall
Talk
Cry
Sing
Love
Win
Know
Cook
Dream
Go

Guess What?

I ate your apology for lunch
I smoked your smile into the sun
I flicked your frankly frozen face
I jumped your bare bones just for fun
I sucked the sour from your sloppy soul
I tore down the signs in total totality
I quit calling her magical Mandy
I burned all the boring branches brilliantly
I hope it doesn't feel too fiery forever

User Pencils

They run out before you use them
Orange, brown, and gold delusion
Ridges with no altruism
Uneven led with permanency
Scribble tracing erasable indecision
Quintessential dried-up shmuck erasers
Almost twelve inches shorter than you
Burp only in front of others
They wannabe number two next to God

He Made Her Fatter

He knew what she represented
He screwed with her ears anyway
He pinned the tail on her problems
He called her down from what matters
He stole her affection for liberty
He thrived on selling her short
He bought her thirst for provocative problems
He drained his own desperate decisions
He avoided assassination of his own lying liver
He snuck himself inside her beliefs and morals
He vehemently destroyed her perpendicular vision
He pressed her ultimate life purpose down to the bottom
of the barrel
He vexed her permanent mailing address
He won't remember her middle name
He took the easy way out through her mouth

Check Me

I'm afraid of singing bears
I talk beneath my mouth
I laugh when no one is around
I was born between prison bars
I wiped the orange out of the sun
I ripped the biggest fart hole in the moon
I gently told his mom what she thinks
I dream of bigger dreams
I slapped my own soul into submission
I will never be a person of temporal fame

Drunk Trees

They drive into our phones
They see sexual indecency up-close
They wake the sleeping whoremongers
They taste the blood of childhood thugs
They provide an end to step ten
They grow in sanctuaries of broken love
They reach just past six feet of instincts
They close the door on carpool chores
They bring dad into his biggest misery
They leap when the buzzards buzz
They yoke the dead with the living

Happy Me

It's the part of me that lives inside of you
It's the part of me that shatters past
all that shouldn't matter
It's the joyful me that offers overflowing humility
It's the me that wishes her son were three
It's the me that is ok with not liking chocolate ice cream
It's the me that jokes about not winning the spelling bee
It's the me that prefers less notoriety
It's the me that covers ugly seas
It's the me that partakes in life building bullying
It's the me that fears the other me

Trashy Me

I will bite the hell out of you
I will punch your ears with unbearable truth
I will leave laughs in your belly for days and weeks
I will not care how I look at you
I will claim there's no more money
I will detest your fake pint of generosity
I will poke my own buttons
I will entertain unholy trends
I will forget my own value
I will throw more fire at the water
I will be dignified minus three
I will gush obscenities
I will arrive for every other blink

It All Makes Cents

He was hit in the face
His mom even acknowledged the disgrace
His mom spat ego flattery into his digestive tract
He puked his mom's self-effacing calamity,
into his self-made identity
She laughed behind his face
He picked up an emotional hammer
She used his dad as her best defense
He went ahead and choked on her lack of dignity
She kept striving to live by a false exterior
He lived his life pointing the finger at the wrong people
She lifted the waste of space basket,
that was her marriage
He ran past his own purple hearted matter
She grew more and more unhappy in her mind
He fondled himself to sleep
She never went to bed

Sun of A Nun

He borrowed other people's thumbs
He increased the temperature of the self-correction oven
He thought about committing rape,
when set to medium heat
He promised to watch over his liver
He forced the dark to come out,
by sinking to his all-time low
He tripped over his own prideful fall
He awoke to Linda playing with his Nintendo
He sabotaged clever conversations
He will not live past his mother

Confused Mermaids

They don't give a flare
They wear rainbow freedom in their hair
They smell as salty as a woke fin
They swallow laughter from the fresh air
They use artificial intelligence to do their make up
They drink dilated frozen lemonade
They cause shrinkage in the pants
They live for swimming's sake
They watch your liberty go down the ocean's drain
They steer left from the left wave
They will not hold the door with their tail
They splash bitterness onto dry land

Kind of Ridiculous

I'm not yours
You're not mine
Time and energy don't always combine
It makes no sense for flies to temporarily exist
Open your eyes to his hit list
You're next in line to dine in the fire
Breakfast is dinner and dinner is lunch
I have more than a small hunch
Enemies belong in the front seat
Let them stay unbuckled for the ride
Story tellers never reach their final destination

Horoscope

Shove bogus news down my virtual throat
Wipe my mind with predictive flattery
Jump my bones into naïve submission
Pop my hope for things to work out
Prick my thumb to say something dumb
Everything you hear is not for fun

Price Tags

Will it cost me-
ten oxfords?
my open November?
my childish banter?
my haircut appointment?
my one phone call home?
my mental leftovers?
my cellular data?
my drunk laughter?
my seat at the table?
my badge of fake honor?
my husband's never will I ever?
my premier location?
my first-class seat?

So

What comes next?
What is under that dress?
What sends clouds and rain?
What is up his butt?
What made her throw up?
What was that smell?
What if they failed?
What can't be seen?
What is the fuss about?
What was poured in his cup?
What came off the bus?
What will it be?

Treasures From Heaven

They hail down from indecision
They come after the messiest lesson
They appear when you keep believing
They smell like holy waters
They place you in second
They show you why he came
They leave you praying for more
They fill your heart with splendor
They lift your head off the floor
They drizzle grace on your mistakes
They teach you how to run your race
They wipe the dust off your heart
They bring you closer to the Lord

Double Vision

It sends you into outer space
It makes you skip across the moon
It takes your common-sense particles
It steers your mind towards Jupiter
It catapults regret up Uranus
It dents your starry ideals
It crushes the air into lethal lung meteorites
It helps you see clear past the sun

The Dumbest

Piece of shit
House of lies
Saul of Tarsus
Whale full of salad
Exposed tree roots
Clown from triple Hell
Ground I've never walked on
Apple grower
Parenthetical lover
Sounds on Sandy Lane
Face full of blame
Don't take his name in vain
Worthless adult video games

Run In the Rain

School is out today,
so other people won't drive your nervous system insane

Better not miss the rain
The rain kills that which is dead

Plan to drink the rain all night and day
Force yourself to recognize the rain as anger

Running represents loss of aim
The rain drops release all his never-ending pain
It's best to stomp gently through all the puddles of
shame

Chinese-Japanese

Look at me
Try not to blink
Break their dreams
Believe their whys
Find even more reasons rise in their eyes
Chop their fish just to exist

Homeless By Choice

Don't be quick to give what isn't needed
Some folks choose the street on purpose
Let them figure out their own dysfunction
It's not cruel to withhold assistance for withholding is assistance
Tuff love might just be the fix they need
Beggars enable their own heart wrenching self-destruction

A handout won't help
They will just keep begging
There has to be a real solution
Not giving actually gives what's needed
Think about who made their decisions
Homeless bondage isn't your load to carry

Forever Fantasy

Sleeping smiles glittering timeless stars
Flowers breathe endless dancing change
Knights swoop fairies gently over fire
Goth lights blind cheerful toads
Dragonfly Hall music deliciously covers time
Everyone smelled like warm fruitful elixir
Dragons want unicorn costumes with bells
Music festivals continually bless queen mermaid
Mythical vacation windows offer wonderous mental play
time

Happy Wednesday

Humpty Dumpty sat on a moth
Humpty Dumpty swallowed them all
All the botulinum and all the plastic surgery,
couldn't make Humpty twenty-one ever again

Forensic Files

His heart was demolished by fear
His lungs were emptied by lies
His intestines were full of worry rocks
His liver still gave liquor quivers
His testicles shriveled at the sound of her name

His legs became more unsymmetrical every birthday
His feet presented with disjointed laughter
His eye sockets bulged with pent up frustration
His hair was contaminated at the roots
His skull was invisibly fractured
His mind contained ideas that were his only friends

Temptation Station

The pole
The kitchen
The tub
The bar
The curb
The closet
The floor
The backdoor
The backseat
The movies
The bathroom
The bedroom
The couch
The stairs
The elevator
The hallway
The garden

Happy Sunday

No cussing
No lying
No working
No dancing
No sex
No laughing
No smoking
No joking
No drinking
No spanking
No smiling
No cooking
No creating
No cleaning
No dreaming
No complaining
No touching
No painting
No mowing
No talking
No Chick Fil-A

Fluffy Bitches

They have warm hands of flour
They have hearts that melt chocolate
They have smiles that eat your words
They have backsides in all kinds of proportions
They have sandwiches when they're late
They have cankles made of oil and butter
They have the guts to lick the plate
They have recipes of what not to eat
They have rolls they got off the stove
They have cushion, but do the pushing

Amaze Balls

I'm off that leash
I lost those pounds
I bought that house
I took twenty-one of those pills
I finally quit that job

My friend got caught in those lies
My mom divorced that sleaze
My driveway is behind those knees
My hair is always that important
My heart needs those gravitations

You actually took that bath
You drove right into those dreams
You fought that urge to die
You ignored that jerk who laughed

They grabbed those because they're free
They punched that liver with shots
They smelled those piles of crap
They loved that dog too much
They never saw those open gates

Boys vs. Girls

Balls	Calm	Xenocentric
Boobs	Chaotic	Xenial
Friends	Egotistical	Yoke
Foes	Eager	Yolk
Tall	Austere	Zaddy
Trusting	Amiable	Zaftig
Pride	Horny	
Pleasing	Hungry	
Drive	Jeering	
Driven	Jealous	
Gross	Kick	
Gitty	Kiss	
Silly	Negate	
Serious	Nag	
Masculine	Obliging	
Manipulated	Obedient	
Loud	Quest	
Listener	Queen	
Inclusive	Umpire	
Inviting	Unicorn	
Rebellious	Visualize	
Refined	Validate	

Cesar's Penis

Uncircumcised
Unruly
Unholy
Unforgiving
Unclean
Undersized
Untouchable
Unhinged
Unbelievable
Unloving
Unmeasurable
Unpredictable
Unfair
Unaware
Unlawful
Uncomfortable
Unappealing

Didn't You Know?

Money don't grow on fleas
Some flowers are eighty years old
Santa Claus will never be real
The tooth fairy doesn't eat teeth
Angel got bit, not stung by a bee
Tom doesn't know Harry or Dick
Basketballs don't drool
Cremation is considered an abomination
Southern is sometimes sweeter
Northern prefers to look Eastern
Western boots ain't always cute
Shut doesn't go down
Rap is organic smooth talk
Make up doesn't change a thing
An erection never lasts forever
Magic is better left in the fridge
Nipples come in big and small
Grown up doesn't mean grown
Hot air kisses the toilet

Back That Thing Up

Pickled peppers
Zesty flavor
Taco salad
Mix it together
White rice
Boiled nice
Slider sauce
Standing next to the boss
Mashed cake
I like how it tastes
Eggs of stone,
lost their throne
Hold the mayo
We're going to San Diego
It's going to be fuego

Wanna Play?

Do things my way
Save the best for first
Plagiarize my guitar
Open blind people's hearts
Grow weeds in concrete
Override what they don't say
Hold the door on their blank face
Wash their name from the sand
Eat the short fries
Drown in a pimp's cup
Rip the mask off their bank account
Pet my dog while he goes poop
Let your brows come together
Wrap the gift for the stripper
Countdown from your last mistake

Sea Tooth

Sushi wushi
Wishy washy
Sushi badooshee
Want your mommy?
Sushi calooshi
Say when!
Sushi pooshie
I'll tell you the truthsies
Sushi limooshi
Can't take it?!
Sushi tushi
Never forget
Sushi gamblushi
Wet buffets

Crush Me

Into pieces
Into walls
Into jaws
Into bars
Into pillows
Into sand
Into mirrors
Into lemonade
Into bison
Into rivers
Into watermelon
Into splinters
Into pie
Into cars
Into nails
Into bushes
Into dinosaurs
Into maltodextrin
Into cans
Into fragments
Into you

I Could

Just fade
Just drive
Just give up
Just give in
Just leave
Just run
Just vanish
Just explode
Just scream
Just cry
Just lie
Just try
Just fly
Just borrow
Just laugh
Just pray
Just stay
Just pause
Just breathe
Just dream
Just believe
Just trust

No Hope

Sad
Down
Afraid
Left
Rejected
Turn
Betrayed
Around
Lust
Blink
Dying
Twice

The Year

You changed
You won
You froze
You saw
You learned
You found
You fought
You hurt
You survived
You thrived
You reconnected
You synthesized
You wondered
You shared
You gave
You overcame

Stinks

Your breath
Your hair
Your clothes
Your butt
Your balls
Your house
Your mind
Your dog
Your cat
Your idea
Your feet
Your bed
Your submission
Your voice
Your food
Your trash
Your kid
Your name
Your swing
Your mom

Spring-a-ling

Time moves forward
The sun moves backward
Green pollenated wind gives cars serious blow jobs
Trees grow leaves on fleek
Humans sneeze for all sorts of treason
Perennials make cameo appearances
Birds sing their balls off
Parks overload with depressed moms
Strawberry short cake hits the hips
Kids whine about wanting to take a dip
Windows open releasing people's business
Now you know why it's called March Madness

Bad Rappers

Grovel at Satan's feet
Ignore the heart of the beat
Lead listeners onto the streets
Dangle gold carrots for fun
Take little digs at their mom
Wish their barber wore a thong
Sport a grille to disguise their pain
Flash money when they hear their name
Cuss like sailors and feel no shame
Ride with loud music to block the truth
Use desperate women to tickle their ego
Pimp their dog without limits
Fight their battles with more than loaded words
Create reasons for suspicious intrusions
Drown listeners with poisonous lyrics

Wannabe?

Funny?
Please!
Healthy?
Sure!
Loved?
Ok!
Prompted?
Someday!
First?
Chill!
Serious?
Way!
Athletic?
Really!
Single?
Cheat!
Young?
Laugh!
Dead?
Cry!
Forgotten?
Lie!

Evil Ones

You thought I would always overlook,
all that you took for granted
The first mistake you made was project shame

Then, you lowered my name
Cough up those credentials quietly
Second mistake you made was lying

After that, you drove the knife in further
False promises can't erase blood stains
Third mistake you made was spread self-righteous
propaganda

At this point, you thought you won
Entitled is your middle name
The last time you devour, you will face truth

You are the broken soul
You were the problem
You live for you

Mushy Gushy

How I love to look at you,
especially when your eyes are their deepest blue

If only you knew all the feelings you cause within me
How I long to always be with you

I could make the scariest case-
for why we shouldn't separate

What He brings together,
is always something that gets better and better

Weather the storms,
and love will keep blooming

Peace will overflow the shores,
coating the prettiest of sea shells

Singing we will do,
but they will be nowhere near clandestine tunes

Thank you for indulging in cataclysmic truths by exploring the poetic works found in the pages of this poetry book. This set of poems is dedicated to my father who never lived long enough to share his own truths with the world. Love and peace to all readers; in particular, those with an appreciative understanding of expressive language art.

"If you tell the truth, you don't have to remember anything."
                    -Mark Twain

www.ingramcontent.com/pod-product-compliance
Lightning Source LLC
Chambersburg PA
CBHW071007280626
47160CB00015B/2061